Graphic design and illustrations: Zapp
Story adaptation: Robyn Bryant

© 1994 Tormont Publications Inc.
  338 Saint Antoine St. East
  Montreal, Canada   H2Y 1A3
  Tel. (514) 954-1441
  Fax (514) 954-5086

ISBN 2-89429-504-9

Printed in China

RAPUNZEL

TORMONT

There once lived a couple who longed to have a child. Finally, their wish came true.

As the wife waited for her child to be born, she sometimes stared out the window at the garden next door. In it grew some delicious-looking rapunzel lettuce.

But the garden belonged to a witch, and no one dared to go into it.

After a time, the wife could think of nothing but that lettuce. She grew paler and paler. Finally, her worried husband decided to sneak into the garden after dark and pick some.

His wife ate it all, but it only made her want more. So the husband went back to the garden.

This time, the witch caught him. "How dare you steal my rapunzel!" she screeched. The terrified husband told her of his wife's craving. "Take all the lettuce you want, then," said the witch. "But in return, you must give me the child."

The poor man agreed.

As soon as the child
was born, the witch took it
away to raise as her own.
She called the baby girl
Rapunzel.

Rapunzel grew to be so beautiful that the witch decided no one else must ever see her beauty.

So when the child reached the age of twelve, the witch shut her in a tower deep in the forest. The tower had no door. When the witch came to visit, she called, "Rapunzel, Rapunzel, let down your hair."

Then the girl threw her long braid out the window, and the witch climbed it to the tower room.

A few years later, a prince happened to be riding in the forest and heard Rapunzel singing to amuse herself.

He was drawn
to her sweet voice,
but could find no
way into the tower.

The prince couldn't stop thinking about the voice in the tower, and went back every day.

One day, from his hiding place, he saw the witch call, "Rapunzel, Rapunzel, let down your hair." Then the braid was let down. "If that's the rope to climb, I'll try it," he decided.

The prince called "Rapunzel Rapunzel, let down your hair," and climbed the long braid.

Rapunzel was at first frightened, as she had never before seen a man. But he explained how he had been drawn to her voice, and asked her to marry him. Rapunzel liked him better than the witch, and agreed.

But she had no way to leave the tower. The prince promised to bring a ball of silk each time he came to visit, so that she could weave a ladder and escape.

The prince visited every night, and Rapunzel kept his visits a secret. But one day, she blurted out to the witch, "Why are you so much heavier than the prince?"

"How dare you trick me!" the witch screamed, and in a fury, she cut off Rapunzel's long hair.

$\mathcal{S}$he used a magic spell to send Rapunzel to a far-off land. Then she tied the long braid to the windowsill and waited for the prince. When he arrived, she cackled, "Your little songbird is gone, and you will never see her again!"

The prince was beside himself with grief, and leapt from the tower window.

He landed in a thornbush, which scratched his eyes. He was blinded!

*H*ow
would he ever
find Rapunzel
now?

$\mathcal{F}$or months, the
prince wandered blindly
through the forest, weeping.

One day, by chance, he heard someone singing a beautiful but sad song. He recognized the voice at once, and ran towards it, calling her name.

As Rapunzel rushed into his arms, a strange thing happened. Her tears of joy fell on his eyes, and he could see again.

And so Rapunzel married the prince, and they lived happily ever after.